THE CUCKOO CAPERS

First published in India by HarperCollins *Children's Books* 2025
An imprint of HarperCollins *Publishers*

HarperCollins Publishers India, Cyber City, Building 10-A,
Gurugram, Haryana-122002, India

www.harpercollins.co.in

2 4 6 8 10 9 7 5 3 1

P-ISBN: 978-93-6989-372-0
E-ISBN: 978-93-6989-185-6

Series design by Denise Antao
Layout and design in Quicksand 10pt/16 by Isha Nagar

Printed and bound at Thomson Press India Ltd

*

HarperCollins Publishers, Macken House, 39/40 Mayor Street Upper,
Dublin 1, D01 C9W8, Ireland

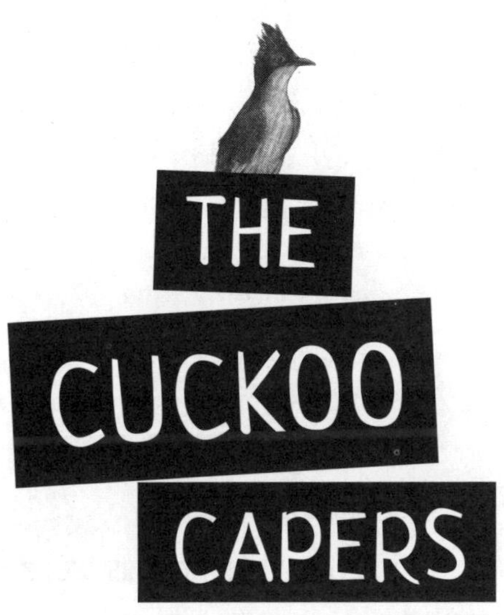

BIJAL VACHHARAJANI

ILLUSTRATED BY
CANATO JIMO

No frogs or other animals were harmed in the making of this book.

CHAPTER 1

The Decent Folks of Decent Apartments

The Mehta-Kamble house—A 203, Decent Apartments—was not known for being a calm one. Sounds of different kinds and volumes erupted from that household all the time.

Like the constant clatter of utensils, which sounded like there was a game of Jenga being played with them. Or the nonstop laughter of all sorts. Chuckles. Guffaws. Giggles. It was like a dictionary of laughs lived in there.
Bollywood films were played on loop, especially Shah Rukh Khan movies.

Alas, the walls of Decent Apartments weren't decently thick. So when the films, utensil clatter and laughter paused, you could hear oohs and aahs and arguments that went on forever about something strange. It wasn't about politics or school or office. It was—

'That was definitely a wagtail.'

'I heard an ashy prinia today.'

'Ah, the call of the *Prinia socialis*. So telling.'

'Ooh look! Praying mantis!'

'Hey see? Jumping spider.'

'That's a white eye.' 'No, it's not.' 'It totally is.'

'Shall we watch *Swades* again?'

'*Cinnyris asiaticus, Cinnyris asiaticus!* On the *Peltophorum pterocarpum*.' (Translation: Purple sunbird, purple sunbird! On the Copperpod tree.)

All the neighbours knew what the Mehta-Kamble household was talking about. It was about birds, bees and insects—everything flora and fauna. And sometimes films.

Most of them did not mind the noise. Except for one family.

At first, the Sharmas of Flat A103 bought personal noise-cancelling headphones for each family member. They even installed double-pane windows to shut the noise out. Then they filed several complaints with the society secretary, Sadaf Aunty, and on the building WhatsApp group. Finally, they moved lock, stock and barrel from the city itself.

The rest of Decent Apartments was relieved. Especially because—

When not writing scripts for TV serials, Nilesh Kamble would pop around with a batch of freshly baked, palm oil-free, hazelnut chocolate-stuffed, triple chocolate-chip cookies. He would trill a song while waiting to take his plate back, and made terrible dad jokes, much to the horror of his children, Subhir and Kiana. Example: When Subhir got a C- in a test, his dad made apple crumble and said, stay strong and don't crumble. SIGH.

Dr Kinjal Mehta-Kamble would be available for free advice on a surprising range of ailments—a fungus-laden toe or a pesky cold that wouldn't go—and had excellent remedies for aches and pains. (But beware, if you went to her with a fake ailment, she'd give you vile-tasting stuff to drink!) Also, she would write up a note and you could give it to your teacher and miss school on the day of the history test. (She'd do it for a lot of children, but not her own. Which both Subhir and Kiana agreed was totally unfair.)

Catrina was world famous in Decent Apartments for giving leg rubs to the neighbours. The ginger cat was the beloved of everyone, including Mr Mafatlal who abhorred all sorts of animals, but made an exception for Catrina. With her litany of soft purrs, she had captured everyone's hearts, and they kept a bit of food for her in their homes, as a result of which she was as round as a panda's tummy.

Whenever Nilanjana Mehta visited her daughter, she was a familiar figure in the building society, power-walking every evening in a crisp cotton sari with toothpaste-white sports shoes. Kinjal's mother was full of smiles and toffee, and she would even kick the football back whenever it sauntered in her path. She also plied her grandkids with avian stories of which she had an unending supply.

Together they were the perfect go-to people for when you wanted an A+ on your project about the natural world because they knew everything about tigers, tapirs and tarantulas. *Panthera tigris*, *Tapiridae*, and *Theraphosidae*, as Ma called them.

Which is why Subhir and Kiana couldn't understand why their pleasantly not-calm house was suddenly unpleasant and not calm.

CHAPTER 2

A Storm on the Horizon

Dad had stopped baking cookies and brownies and was constantly making healthy granola bars that seemed to have more oatmeal than nuts. Worse, there wasn't a single chocolate chip to be found inside the stodgy concoction! Just yesterday, he had mumbled about buying beetroot to make beet-ginger granola bars. Listening to him, Subhir had turned more purple than any organic beetroot.

Meanwhile, Ma looked like she needed one of her own prescriptions because she was constantly grumbling, as though she was the one with the aches now. And, instead of chasing Kiana to clean up her messy desk, she was lying on the couch, endlessly watching reruns of *Anupaama*, and shaking her fist at all the characters except Anupamaa. In fact, they had stopped watching movies. They had even missed the latest SRK blockbuster!

News had also been turned off ever since they saw a bunch of politicians floating thermocol sheets on Tulsi Lake to stop the surface water from evaporating in the extremely summery summer. The sheets had disintegrated into thermocol blobs and had further polluted the lake. Money had to be spent on cleaning up the lake. 'Waste of tax money,' Nani had muttered.

Nani had stopped going on walks, groaning that it was too hot, and she had a throbbing blister on her little toe, which Ma had mostly ignored except to give her a tub of petroleum jelly. Nani kept threatening to go back home to Jamnagar, but then moaned and did not.

Catrina had completely stopped leaving the house, and the entire Decent Apartments' from blocks A to D, was missing her. Makhija Aunty had made fish fry last Sunday, and even that aroma hadn't enticed Catrina out of the house. She just lay flat on the marble floor, right under the fan.

'This can't go on.' Subhir miserably crumbled a granola bar and poked at it. 'I am a growing child. I want a balanced meal of chocolate, cookies, and brownies. And potatoes.'

'That is not a balanced meal,' Dad said, as he stormed out of the kitchen. He tugged off his apron and dramatically tossed it into the laundry bin. He then went back and retrieved it—it wasn't dirty enough to merit a tumble in the washing machine. 'Why do I even bother! There is nothing balanced anymore. I give up. It's too hot, I will not cook. I am the one being baked. And not even into a nice cake.' He plopped onto the sofa where Ma was lying down. She grunted, shifted her feet to make room for him, and continued watching her serial. Dad passed her an ice cube, which she rubbed onto her forehead while he crunched on another one.

Every nine minutes Ma, Dad and Nani would shuffle out and pick up a pair of binoculars—they were laid out neatly on their second-floor windowsill to scan the skies. They would then shake their heads, sigh, and go back to their chopping, bingeing and ice-crunching. Dad would shake his fist at a pigeon.

Nani let out a loud tsk-tsk and returned to chopping lady's fingers while glaring at her daughter and son-in-law. She looked like she was ready to chop off someone's fingers. Every few seconds, she would wipe her hands and look at her phone at the many 'good morning' WhatsApp messages from her different groups—Mehta Family, Garden Group, Walking Group, Mehta NRI Family, Yoga Group—and respond to them with an appropriate photo, reaction or GIF. Then she said, 'In our days, the . . . '

Kiana sighed too. She mopped her forehead and stifled a scream that was building up in her throat. If she heard one more time how in their days of yore (and bore) her grandmother could count on the rains to come exactly on such and such day or even one more tadaang tadaang tadaang from the TV, she was going to scream and scream and scream.

The summer had already been awful, with temperatures soaring up to 55 degrees Celsius and heat waves rocking the whole country. Now, it was July, and there wasn't a rumble in the sky. Already, their summer holidays had been ruined, and in the last week of vacation, they were still sweltering and sweating. Worst, Catrina refused to sit on any of their laps . . . and who could blame her, it was so hot! The feeling was entirely mutual—no one wanted a warm fur ball on their lap.

There was only one storm brewing in all of Mumbai, and that was in the Mehta-Kamble household.

'This can't go on,' Kiana told her brother. At the age of eleven, Subhir was older than her by two years, but he constantly behaved like the younger one. Firstly, he was very short, and Kiana was unusually tall for her age, which didn't help matters. Plus, he still had chubby cheeks, so everyone assumed he was the younger one and plied him with chocolates as a bribe to let them pinch his cheeks.

'Excuse me, I just said that!' Subhir pointed out, indignantly. He had found a lone raisin in the granola and had cheered up.

'No, this!' Kiana pointed at their family. She lowered her voice and said, 'They are such annoying grumps.'

'They are! Even you are.'

'I so am not.'

'You are!'

'Uff, stop distracting me.' Kiana glared at her brother. How was he older than her, how! 'We need to somehow get rain.'

'Get rain mhanje? How will we *get* rain?'
'Mhanje, we need to go looking for that cuckoo. Sitting here is not helping anyone. Especially them.' She stared at the grown-ups and shook her head.

Subhir looked at his sister like she had turned into a cuckoo. Who could blame her? The heat had

addled everyone's brains, turning them into mush. Not even delicious mush like when your strawberry and chocolate bubble gum ice cream melted into a puddle that's the right amount of cold. Brain mush was yucky and tiring. He wondered if he should get her ice cream. Ooh, he could also do with some.

'Kiana, I think you should lie down. I will make the fan faster,' he said in what he hoped was a calming tone. It was the one the school principal used on him when trying to get him to confess to a prank. Like the time he put fart spray in the staffroom or when he flipped the screens on all the computers in the lab so that they were upside down.

So far, the Mehta-Kamble house had resisted buying an air conditioner (we must be socially responsible, Dad had declared), so fans, ice cubes and cold showers were the only options. Only, cold showers were now limited to one a day because of the water supply cuts.

'It's already fast!' Kiana snapped. She couldn't understand how Subhir didn't understand what was happening. 'And looking for the cuckoo is the only option. Once the sun goes down a bit, we're going for a walk.'

A WALK! The two words that Subhir feared the most, along with beetroot, detention and conjugated verbs. It was 55 degrees outside! Plus, out of the whole family, he was the only one who was not obsessed with birds and insects and trees. The only buzzing he wanted to be surrounded by was the one that came from his games. He always slept in while the family went on long—and what sounded like difficult—hikes and trails and expeditions. When the family went on safaris, he was content to see everything from the relative comfort of the jeep or, even better, stay back in the room, playing on his Game Boy. He was really not a fan of snakes and lizards; birds were all right but to him they were just blobs on trees. He couldn't figure out how his entire family knew that that blob was a pied kingfisher or a golden oriole. Or which tree was home to some bark gecko. He didn't want to know, thank you very much.

But Subhir knew that once his younger sibling had made up her mind, no one could do anything. Well, that was true of every single member of the Mehta-Kamble household, especially Catrina. Which is why usually Subhir just agreed to what Kiana said. He hoped that she would forget. He was exceptionally good at forgetting, so he encouraged that trait in others.

CHAPTER 3
Walking the Talk

But come early evening, Kiana was all strapped up in her walking boots and ready with a straw hat and a giant water bottle the size of a lauki.

With a huge sigh, Subhir tied his shoelaces. He watched warily as Kiana strode up to their parents and grandparent and said, 'Get up. Now. Let's go.'

The three of them barely looked at her.

Kiana switched off the television.

'Kiana!' Ma whimpered.

'GET UP!' The scream that Kiana had been bottling up inside her finally spilt out. Ma frowned. Dad looked startled. Nani shook her head. 'Please, please!' Kiana added quickly. Rudeness was not tolerated in the Mehta-Kamble household.

Kiana then prodded Ma, Dad and Nani until, finally annoyed by the action, they all slowly got up.

'Take your binoculars, wear your shoes, and come on. You cannot just sit around. CHALO.'

Dad, Ma and Nani shrugged. It was better than just sitting around, Kiana was right.

Just behind Decent Apartments was Beauty Van. Newcomers to Mumbai often thought it was a place to buy beautiful vans and other automobiles. They would arrive there with a fat file of papers and even fatter cheques and would instead find tall trees, shrubs, and absolutely no cars allowed inside.

Beauty Van was a city forest, one of the last remaining patches of green there. The city now had more golf courses than forests but that's beside the point. Beauty Van was a popular hotspot for school trips, couples and families. It was also one of the reasons that the residents of Decent Apartments had greater coucals and atlas moths as visitors, and slept to the chirps of frogs and crickets at night.

Beauty Van had once been home to leopards. But the leopards got irritated by everyone in the city and by the lack of water. So, they left to find better neighbours and abundant water, making the forest feel a tad lonely.

But today it was being visited by Kiana and Subhir and their family. Except for Catrina, of course.

As they paid the ticket price and stepped into the Van, they suddenly found themselves relaxing. It was noticeably cooler than outside. Tense shoulders became un-tense and teeth stopped being ground to stubs.

Ma walked up to an Indian rosewood tree and touched its trunk. 'Hello *Dalbergia sissoo*,' she whispered softly. Nani was already stooped, hand on her back, and staring at a sheet and funnel web spider. Dad had his binoculars glued to his eyes as he stumbled forward, mumbling, 'Greater racket-tailed drongo . . . Flowerpecker . . . Spotted dove . . .' '*Dicrurus paradiseus* . . . *Dicaeum erythrorhynchos* . . . *Spilopelia chinensis*,' Ma whispered alongside.

'Aha!' Subhir said.

Kiana giggled. Finally, the penny, or rather the paisa, had

dropped for her brother. She took a sip of water and looked around her. The park was empty—there were hardly any visitors today. A lot of the rich people had run away to cooler climates. The rest of them were left to suffer and complain or just get on with it, which is what most people did.

'We're here to look for the pied cuckoo!'

‘Well done, Sherlock.’ Kiana rolled her eyes.

Every year, the Mehta-Kambles impatiently waited for the arrival of the Jacobin cuckoo aka the pied cuckoo aka the chatak aka *Clamator jacobinus*. Sightings of the mohawk-toting bird meant that monsoon was around the corner.

Kiana loved the cuckoo. After all, the black-and-white bird was quite notorious. Like most cuckoos, this one laid her eggs in other birds’ nests, leaving all the caregiving responsibilities to another bird family. Plus, the bird was quite a traveller! When Kiana grew up, she wanted to see the world, and like the chatak, she too wanted to go to southern Africa. She had heard there were whales and penguins there! Not to mention cheetahs and lions and giraffes! She had a wish list of animals that she wanted to meet, which was as long as a giraffe’s neck. But first, she wanted to see all the animals, birds and insects of India.

Whenever the chatak was first sighted, Dad would bake up a storm, Ma would put on music and the whole family would dance like they were in some Bollywood joint family saga. But this year, the piu-piu call of the bird had eluded them.

That is why the family had been down in the dumps. Apart from the heat and the no-show of the clouds. Which is why, Kiana had taken matters into her extremely able hands and hoped that they could look for the cuckoo in the shrubs of the Van. Where else would a bird go if she was visiting the city?

Off they went, feeling like they were in a Michael Rosen book going on a cuckoo hunt, armed with binoculars, gross granola bars and mosquito repellent. Subhir gingerly stepped exactly where everyone walked, trying not to think of leeches and other blood-sucking, ear-nestling, venom-injecting creepies and crawlies. Even though his parents had tried to explain how most of these creatures preferred to stay away from humans, he still felt his heart beating in his ears when he was forced to walk a trail.

He couldn't help but wonder why they were looking for a bird that couldn't even be bothered to build her own nest! Yes, she was a harbinger of monsoon and all, but surely there were other ways of tracking rain, like looking at the clouds or seeing the weather forecast online. All of it was perfectly possible from the safety of their own home! Which had fans.

'I know what you're thinking.' Kiana sidled up to her brother. 'Don't! Look at how excited they are.' Subhir couldn't help but agree.

For the next thirty-two minutes, no one spoke. They looked up and down, left and right and in all directions to look for the bird. 'They are found in shrubs, also low-level branches, so can't be that high, can it?' Ma wondered out loud.

Every flutter of black and white—whether it was a red-vented bulbul, a deflated football, or a plastic bag—caused a flutter in their hearts.

But luck wasn't on their side.

'This is rubbish!' Dad finally said, packing away his binoculars before he was tempted to throw them in a fit of rage. He picked up a stray plastic bottle and put it in the garbage bag they always carried with them. 'This is also rubbish. There is no cuckoo. Maybe they've gone extinct too, like the golden toad and that Australian rat, what was it called?'

'Bramble Cay melomys,' Kiana helpfully offered, while Ma added, '*Melomys rubicola*.'

'Yes, that! All gone! I'm sure the cuckoo is also gone. Udan choo from this Earth. Serves us right.'

Nani shook her head and began breathing deeply. She fished around in her purse and removed her phone, which for that last half hour and two minutes hadn't been glued to her hand. She began scrolling through her WhatsApp messages rapidly, and muttering, 'No signal, no signal, need signal.'

Ma meanwhile looked like she wanted to get back to her serial. Her fingers were moving rapidly as if desperately trying to press play on a phantom remote control.

Nani had raised her phone arm, the other on her back, and was standing on tiptoe trying to catch some network. Subhir gently pulled her back down and held her hand. He squeezed it, and she squeezed it back. He suddenly felt less scared about the elements, and more worried about his family.

He looked at his sister and saw the same worry reflected in her eyes. They had finally managed to—well, Kiana had—drag the grown-ups out of the house and now they were going to fall apart again. Worse, Subhir was braving the elements for them, and they hadn't shown a single sign of appreciation. Hmpf.

Subhir led Nani towards a lichen-covered tree stump, and helped her sit down.

'We need rain,' Ma said. Dad nodded sagely.

Nani started breathing in and out even more deeply. She stared at her phone again, as if coaxing a network bar into being. 'I should go back home where there is network,' she muttered.

'Let's make it rain!' Dad said.

'Yes!' Ma beamed at her husband as if he was the smartest human being on the planet.

'Make it?' Subhir asked. He looked at Kiana, who shrugged back. Suddenly the siblings were communicating effortlessly—a thing that had never ever happened in the past.

'What do you mean make it rain, Dad?' she asked, warily. 'This is not one of your TV scripts.'

'We're going to make it rain!' Ma said unnecessarily. She flung her arms around and twirled. She hugged Dad. Nani was nodding away, looking like the Messi bobblehead that Subhir had on his desk.

Now their brains *are* mush, Subhir thought. How did grown-ups become so strange so quickly? Yes, it was hot and not raining, but hare-brained schemes without scientific evidence were very unlike his family. And hares were definitely brainier—what a silly phrase. They were very good at adapting to tropical climates and thriving, Ma had said once. Pea-brained, he meant, pea-brained.

Suddenly the three grown-ups leapt into action. It was the most active they had been all summer. Dad dug out his field notebook, Ma whipped out a pencil, and Nani, who had the best handwriting of them all, began writing furiously. The three grey-streaked heads huddled together.
Thirty-three minutes later, they broke apart from the huddle and said altogether, 'TADAAAAA!'

'So it begins!' Ma announced, as the three of them marched out of the Van.

Subhir grabbed Kiana's hand and hurried after them.

CHAPTER 4

The Mehta-Kamble Planning Commission

The next day was full of meetings and shopping trips. For the grown-ups, that is.

Subhir walked into the kitchen and morosely looked inside the fridge. Kale wilting at its edges. Oat milk that looked suspiciously like clumps of paneer. Broccoli that was more yellow than green. Shopping for groceries was clearly not a priority.

This was not food. At least not for a growing child like him. He pulled out a loaf of bread, which was thankfully not mouldy, and began fixing himself and Kiana some cheese and (free range) egg sandwiches.

'Here.' He slid a plate in front of Kiana, whose nose was buried inside a book about birds. She was surrounded by a mountain of notes and birding books. She looked at the plate—the boiled egg was stuck in clumps to the brown bread, which had come torn in parts and had been pasted back with the help of the cheese spread.

'I didn't think you'd want the oat milk,' Subhir said. 'It smelled funny. Sorry, this is the best I could do. I think if this goes on, I am going to have to learn proper cooking to feed us. They don't look like they need any food.'
The grown-ups in the drawing room seemed like they had been operating on some special battery-fed diet since yesterday.

Catrina leapt onto the dining table, took one look at the plate and turned her back to it.

Subhir went and filled her plate with some cat food. Catrina sprang lightly down and gobbled it up. She then threw a disdainful look at the adult humans, and went back to cleaning herself under the fan.

'See, even she thinks they're behaving strangely!' Subhir said.

So far, the grown-ups had made one long list which was tacked up on the fridge instead of the shopping list that was so direly needed.

THE CUCKOO'S CALLING

- Make frogs, officiate, etc.
- Get the right music
- Order that rainmaking thingamajig. Maybe we can make it? Look online.
- Learn singing
- Find some dance classes. Is it too hot to dance?
- Will fake lightning attract real one? Call TIFR!
- Reach out to Dehradun
- Email and call the Environment Ministry. X at them.
- Be open to new ideas and aces and plans

None of the items on this list made any sense!

'How do you make frogs?' Kiana abandoned her sandwich and bit into an apple instead.

Now, no one could accuse the Mehta-Kamble household adults of being creative. Knowledgeable, yes. But when it came to DIY projects, only Subhir was good at them. Though their father did wield a mean piping bag of icing on cake.

So there he was, holding a giant ball of fondant—alas, not for cake. He was busy moulding two fat green blobs onto a tray. His tongue stuck out a little bit as he concentrated on making a body and then a bumpy head. Limbs followed. Then he switched to an icing bag and began adding black eyes and a strange red tongue.

He ran into the kitchen and began heating sugar. 'Out of my way,' he yelled, holding a hot spatula full of melted sugar. He sat down and began adding spun sugar to one blob's head. It was delicate work, especially in the heat. Dad had switched off the fan so he was sweating buckets and buckets, but he was committed to his task. It was all rather impressive. Weird, but impressive.

'There, done!' He settled back and grinned.

'That's how!' Subhir told Kiana. Their father had made two

adorable-looking frogs, one in a trim tuxedo, the other with a veil made of spun sugar. The two of them held arms (okay, limbs).

'Chalo,' Dad said. 'Let's do this.'

Subhir and Kiana watched open-mouthed as Ma and Nani came up to the frogs and began pronouncing them husband and wife.

'What are they doing? Even I haven't married off my dolls ever,' Kiana whispered.

'What are you asking me for? I didn't marry my dolls off either,' Subhir whispered back. 'I mean, I don't have dolls.'

'Of course you do, I was given them as hand-me-downs,' Kiana said. 'They even have crayon markings on them. And we all know those are yours.'

Subhir pretended not to hear and was busy Googling. 'Aha! They're marrying off frogs. Apparently, it makes the rain gods happy.'

'Well, it's making our parents happy, so maybe it will work?' Kiana said.

'You think we can eat them now?' Subhir asked.

'Gross, I'm not eating married frog fondants.' Kiana made a face. 'You eat them.'

Subhir looked on sadly. He would totally eat them but he wasn't sure how his father would react. Especially since he was looking at the frogs like they were his real children.

The grown-ups shook each other's hands, and then dashed to the window. In unison, they picked up their respective binoculars and stared.

'Look!'

'Pigeon.'

Collective sighs were followed by silence.

'Nothing yet,' Ma said after another ten seconds.

'Give it time,' said Nani. 'The cuckoo has to come all the way from Africa. Do you know how far it is?'

'Of course I do,' Ma snapped back. 'If you remember, I went for a medical conference there five years ago. It's not that far away also.' She paused and then added, 'Okay, but it's not that close.'

'So then, give the cuckoo some time na.'

Dad didn't say anything, he just scanned the horizon, sighed and turned back into the living room. He switched the fan on, increased its speed and plopped himself on the couch.

Catrina jumped onto the coffee table and swallowed the frog bride, veil and all. Dad didn't even say anything. He just closed his eyes.

Two minutes later, Catrina walked up to Subhir and spat out a gloop of green and black. He sighed. Now he would have to clean up this mess as well. Thanks for nothing, Catrina.

CHAPTER 5

Back to the Van

'Why are we back here?' Subhir asked.

It was evening. Having bounced back from the non-appearance of a crest, wing or tail, the Mehta-Kamble household had packed their birding equipment and trooped once again into Beauty Van.

Subhir peered at the forest floor. He was pretty sure someone was stirring beneath a leaf. He quickly stepped back, and promptly fell down. OUCH!

The leaf meanwhile took to the air. Subhir watched as it turned into a butterfly.

'*Melanitis leda*,' Ma pointed out.

'Common evening brown butterfly,' Kiana translated.

'Whatever,' Subhir said. But he couldn't stop staring at the butterfly. Such a good Halloween costume—pretending to be a leaf.

Everything was dry. The leaves crunched beneath their feet. The trees looked sad and mopey, with drooping leaves on sagging branches. Just like the fridge kale. The birds barely trilled, the insects barely buzzed.

'There's the *Ploceus philippinus*,' Ma whispered. 'Poor thing, it nests during the monsoon. It must be waiting and waiting.' Subhir looked at the tiny yellow and brown bird, and a wave of sadness swept over him. Like ice-cream-fallen-on-the-floor-before-you-even-took-a-lick sad. He knew Kiana loved the baya weaver nest. She wanted to grow up and make green homes or some such thing, and kept saying how these birds were extraordinary architects. Subhir was

amazed at how Kiana knew what she wanted to be, even though she was two whole years (and three months) younger than him. He changed his mind almost every day. Adventurer, cartographer, footballer, calligrapher, DJ, gamer, YouTube star—there were too many options.

At last, they reached a spot—a little stream, which was the go-to place for school picnics. Kiana's mouth was a large O. 'When did the stream disappear?' she asked, looking at her parents.

In front of them was a little dip in the ground which was full of smooth pebbles and leaf litter. Above them, the searing blue sky was framed against broccoli-topped trees. Only the leaves were browner than the yellowing broccoli back home. A frog hopped away listlessly, making Subhir jump in alarm again.

'Dried up,' Dad sighed. 'No worries, K! We're going to set it right.'

Subhir stared at all the water bottles they were carrying.

He wondered if the plan was to fill up the stream with the water in them. It would barely make a puddle, no? Well, every drop makes an ocean and all that, so he began twisting the cap off his bottle, when—

‘AAAAAAAAA AAAAAAAAWAAA’
‘AAAAAAAAAA AAAAAAAAAAA AWWWWAAAAAMAAA’
‘AAAAAAAAAAAAAAAA AAAAAAAAAAAAAAAAAA AAWA AAAAAWWWWWWAAAA’

Subhir dropped his water bottle as the adults struck up one of the worst orchestras he had ever heard in his life. The water trickled out, and it made no dent into the stream bed. But a dragonfly did come and rest on the water.

‘RAAAAAAAA AAAAAAA AWAAA’
‘MAAAAAAA AAAAAAAAA AAAAAWWWWAAA AAMAAA’
‘SAAAAAAAAAAAAAAAA AAAAAAAAAAA AAAAAAAAWA AAAAAWWWWWWAAAA’

Kiana covered her ears, shaking her head frantically.

The canopy above them trembled as flocks of birds shot out and flew as far away as they could. The frog that had just hopped suddenly gathered up speed and skittered away. But the adults continued caterwauling without a break.

'STOP! STOP! PLEASE STOP!' Subhir tugged at his parents' shirts frantically. Catching on, Kiana began tugging on Nani's kurta as well.

'WhAAAAAAt!' Ma sang. 'AAAAAAAA—'

'Please! You've scared away all the birds, and everyone.' Subhir pointed at the sky. 'And us.'

'If that cuckoo was coming, she's turned tail and gone back to Africa, I can promise you that.' Kiana glowered at them. Her ears were still ringing with the echoes of their wails. She pressed her ears again to stop them from ringing. Nope, that did not help.

'No, no, don't stop us. We're singing to call the rain clouds. In the ancient times . . .' Nani started.

'NO, NO, NO! That's not going to work. You cannot yell in a forest,' Kiana said.

'We are not yelling,' Dad bristled. 'We know we cannot make noise in a forest. We are singing. REEEREEGAAAAA—'

'That's definitely NOT singing,' Subhir pointed out. 'Even the toad ran away from you. And you also must not sing in a forest. You taught us that!'

Dad pulled out his notebook and crossed out something

vehemently. 'Fine. We have more plans up our sleeve. Our sleeves.' Kiana couldn't help but wonder exactly how long these sleeves were and how many more plans they could hide.

CHAPTER 6

The Common Indian Frog aka the *Polypedates maculatus*

The Common Indian Frog hated his name. What was this nonsense, calling him common? He was VERY unique, he croaked to himself. On top of that, that short boy had called him a toad. He was not a toad. He was a frog. Toads are frogs, but not all frogs are necessarily toads. Did he not even know that much? Annoying human.

But right now, he was hopping away as fast as he could from those five pairs of extremely common (and hairy, eww) legs, making the most horrible noise he had ever heard.

Why weren't the forest guards arresting them?

GUARDS! GUARDS! he croaked. But humans, they never listen, do they?

CHAPTER 7
The Longest Sleeves

'That's not really a sound plan,' Kiana pointed out.

'Well, I think they just like the sound of it,' Subhir said.

The grown-ups had foraged for a hollow bamboo stick in their society's bamboo grove. They then filled it up with raw chana and sealed it on both ends with molten wax. The hot wax had dripped onto their dining table, causing a stain the shape of Africa, which had caused Dad to burst into tears about it being the continent that the cuckoo now seemed to prefer. Then they had paraded the rain stick around the house, making a pleasant swoosh-swoosh rain sound, which, after their caterwauling (not singing), was a relief. But then Ma had started making thunder sounds.

GRRRHHHHGURRRHHHH. She sounded like Catrina when she had an upset stomach.

Catrina had shot straight into Subhir and Kiana's room, deciding it was the safest place for her. She meowed and meowed until Subhir went and switched on the fan.

By then, Kiana had marched up to the thundering-rain-making procession. 'This is just wrong,' she said, crossing her hands and blocking their path.

'Aww,' Dad said, ruffling her hair. 'All you need is a placard, and you would get arrested for exercising your right to dissent.'

'I would not get arrested for that in a democracy,' Kiana said. 'Dissent is allowed. As is the freedom of speech, and because of that, I have to tell you something. This,' she pointed at the rain stick, 'is wrong.'

'Oho! We're doing it wrong?' Ma asked. She immediately began scrutinizing the bamboo stick closely to see if she could hold it differently or correct her posture. She twisted and turned with it, twirling it all around her. 'But I looked it up online.'

'No! You cannot take other cultures' traditions. That's not cool.'

'But we looked online, and so many people . . . '

'Yes, but that's their ritual. You don't know them. You don't belong to those cultures. It's not only embarrassing, but it's . . . ' Kiana looked down at her left hand, where she had written the word down. 'Appro . . . priation. Real uncool.'

Ma went quiet. She looked at Dad, who spluttered, 'What's not cool is that it is not raining.'

'Yes, but you're . . . no, please don't do it like this,' Kiana said. 'Just trust me. Not all answers can be found online. This is not done at all.'

Dad looked puzzled, as did Ma. But Nani understood. She took the rain stick and put it aside. Subhir, who had been hiding with Catrina in their room, came out finally.

After that, the three of them locked themselves up in Nani's room, and both Subhir and Kiana decided it was a good thing—they heard music and uffs and ows and sounds of someone slipping or tumbling, and figured that exercise was good for them. It would release the tension and stress they were all feeling.

The next day was Call to Action Day, aka phone call, email and social media day.

'Hello, where is Megh?' Ma was asking on the phone.

'Ask where's Chatak also—remember, Megh disappeared,' Nani prompted from behind.

'What is happening?' Subhir looked at Kiana, who explained with a long, long sigh, 'They're calling a wildlife organization which tagged two cuckoos with transmitters last year, and are trying to trace where the birds are now.'

Meanwhile, Ma was waving her hand at her mother to be quiet. 'I can't hear them. No, no I mean, where is Megh? Megh, your cuckoo. The one tagged with the solar-powered transmitter.'

Ma listened for a bit and then responded a tad sharply, 'How can you not? I pay my taxes. I have a right to know. In fact, all of us pay our taxes, right on time. Before the due date. Hello, hello?'

Ma put her phone down carefully, though she looked like she also wanted to fling it. The list of things the Mehta-Kamble household wanted to fling was becoming longer by the day. But like binoculars, phones were expensive. Ma often said how much she missed the days when you had those ancient rotary phones, which took forever to dial a number and then caused blisters on the fingers, because you had the satisfaction of banging the phone on someone rude.

'They hung up,' Ma said.

Nani bristled. 'What! We have a right to know.'

'They said to send an email. The person in charge is on leave.'

'Email, shemail,' Dad burst out. He looked up from his laptop. 'I have been mailing the Ministry of Environment, Forest and Climate Change of India for days, and no response. Now, these people are also not going to respond. Everyone must be on leave. All leave should have been cancelled. This is an emergency!' Nani nodded. She had been saying for weeks now that a heat wave emergency should have been declared.

Still, Dad kept refreshing his email every seven minutes. Apart from spam email urging him to buy rainwear, no one seemed to be writing to him. 'I have tweeted them—I mean X'd them—DM'd them on Instagram and left many comments on their Facebook post about saving water, but they don't reply only!'

'That's because you only have some measly 49 followers,' Nani said.

Dad frowned at her.

'I have 156,' she continued. 'I will X to them. That just sounds stupid. I will message them on X. I will also text all my friends and groups. Someone will know someone who knows someone who knows the cuckoo people.' She then turned to Ma and said, 'Kinjal, ask your journalist friend na, what's their name?'

'Arre, Andaleeb's on the medical beat,' Ma said.

'This is an emergency. Even the medical journalists should be writing about it,' Dad said, pounding his fist on the table. An ant quickly veered away, just missing becoming chutney. 'Maybe we can start a petition? Oh, let's start one! I love signing petitions.'

'Wait,' Ma said. 'I know what to do! I will call my conference mates, the ones who live in Cape Town.'

Dad stopped refreshing his email and high-fived Nani. 'What a great idea! Call, call.'

'Yes, and let me ask them where the cuckoo is.'

'Should we even . . . ?' Kiana asked Subhir.

'No point,' Subhir said. He suddenly felt very grown-up. He was mourning the loss of his childhood that seemed to have evaporated in the heat. Just like the stream in the Van. 'They will just shush us or, even worse, give us some calls to make or emails to write.' Kiana had to agree.

Just then, the bell rang. It was Makhija Aunty. She bustled in, a flurry of bright yellow, pink and black. 'We made fish curry. Well, my partner made it, but they are cleaning up so I offered to bring it over.' She shoved a covered bowl into Nani's hands. 'Do you want rice? Then I can—'

'It's too hot to eat,' Dad groaned.

Subhir quickly whisked away the curry, as Ma thanked Makhija Aunty. He, at least, was hungry. And it smelled so good. Makhija Aunty and her partner, André, were excellent cooks.

'What are you all doing?' Makhija Aunty asked, looking at the profusion of mobile phones, laptops and tablets on the dining table. Catrina weaved around her legs. Makhija Aunty bent down to pet the cat, and whispered, 'Come by later. We have kept some yummy treats for you.' She straightened up and continued, 'Conference call?

On a Sunday? You all work too hard. I refuse to work on weekends, I have told my boss. You should also. It's just so unprofessional, I tell you. And not to mention exploitative without overtime.'

If no one stopped Makhija Aunty, she would go on and on like the Kanyakumari–Dibrugarh Vivek Superfast Express which travels for 74 hours across 4,218.6 km through India.

'We are trying to track the cuckoo,' Nani explained quickly. 'They were tagged, you know, so we can check where they are. And trace their journey all the way from—'

Makhija Aunty's eyes glazed over. This was not a unique phenomenon. Until that minute, her kajaled eyes had sparkled with attention. But the moment the Mehta-Kamble household began talking about birds, it was like a gauzy curtain was drawn across them. And it wasn't just with Makhija Aunty.

Subhir did the same. His mouth also slacked a fair bit. Once Kiana had been able to shove a whole cookie in there without him realizing as she talked about the murmuration of rosy starlings. He was rather pleased.

Even Ma's clinic partner, Kiana's friends, and Nani's walking mates—it was amazing how such different people could sport the exact same expression! In fact, all of their WhatsApp groups fell silent when they sent photos of birds they had seen and identified. There would not even be an emoji in response.

'Nice, nice,' Makhija Aunty said, absently. She nodded and began backing out without even turning. Her hands were in front of her as If warding away the words. 'Just give us the bowl later.' She giggled nervously. 'Not in a hurry, you know. We have lots of bowls. So take your time. OK good luck with that chameleon.'

'CUCKOO!' Ma, Dad and Nani yelled.

'Yes, yes, your kaku.' Makhija Aunty quickly skedaddled, shutting the door firmly behind her, just as Catrina slipped through to join her for the promised treat and some much-needed silence.

Dad sighed and refreshed his email yet again. There was just one more bank newsletter suggesting they invest for a rainy day. I would love to invest for a rainy day, Dad thought. But for that it has to rain!

Subhir, meanwhile, was busy heating up millets to go with the curry. He, at least, was happy.

CHAPTER 8

The Domestic Pigeon aka the *Columba livia domestica*

'Coo . . . coo . . . cool gag,' Pigeon 13 bobbed his head at his mate. He loved Pigeon 54 so much, so very much. She was a three-time winner of the Decent Apartment Pooping Contest. She had the most beautiful neck which shone in the sun. And just when he thought she couldn't get coo-er, she had nailed the Decent Apartment Most Annoying Pigeon Contest.

She had taken to fluttering in front of the second-floor window. Every time the homo sapiens lifted up their strange black glinting equipment, she would flap her wings and fly in front of them. The homo sapiens would bob their heads excitedly, just like pigeons. Copy cats! And then they would all start wailing.

That was the coo-est thing he had ever seen.

Pigeon 54 flew to their poop-crusted parapet, and they grasped each other's bills in delight.

CHAPTER 9

Enough!

Nani wailed. Finally, they all gave up staring eagerly at the sky. The cuckoo had not shown up. Instead, every time they pulled out their binoculars, this one pigeon would flap right in front of them. On top of that, there was no sign of clouds either. Not even a pretend one—like smoke from an industry chimney or something.

By now, everyone at Decent Apartments knew something was up in the Mehta-Kamble household. They all steered clear of the family.

If Mr Mafatlal saw them on the way to the sabji wala, he would pretend to be on a phone call.

If André bumped into them while going to pick up a parcel from the security guard, they would lie and say that someone was waiting for them back home. Even though everyone knew Makhija Aunty was in office.

Taking a cue from them, when Catrina saw them, she slipped out and ran to a neighbour's house because she was truly worried they would make her do some rain-calling activity too. She had heard Dad whisper something about 'raining cats and dogs'. Yowl, no thank you.

But they didn't give up. 'We do have one last ace up our sleeve,' Dad announced. 'Sleeves!'

Subhir and Kiana refused to look up from their holiday homework. They didn't want to know, and they didn't want to see this ace which would turn out to be a Joker anyway.

But they didn't have a choice when, yet again, they were marched off to Beauty Van that evening.

'We've taken special permission,' Ma beamed.

'Yes, we have,' Dad beamed even wider.

Nani groaned, but it was her back which was acting up. She was also looking excited as they brandished a piece of paper before the bored security guard's face. He ushered them in and turned back to his cricket commentary. It was an old match, Subhir realized mournfully. All cricket tournaments had been cancelled because of the heat, after a player in the city had fainted on the ground in the first over itself, and there had been a stampede to get refunds on the match.

Kiana was hopeful that this harum-scarum behaviour would end with this stunt. After all, her father had said this was the last ace.

Subhir just wanted to weep at being forced to trek for the third time in a week. That too, in this weather. But, truth be told, he had begun feeling less scared. He couldn't help but love the cheerful purple jacarandas, the lemon-yellow copper pods, and the orange-candy palash trees. But he was so not going to admit it. No need only. He took a deep breath and looked up. The trees already looked familiar to him.

Squelch.

Ewww, he'd just stepped on some poop. Where were the dung beetles when you needed them? Subhir decided to keep his eyes stuck to the forest floor.

'Where are we going?' Kiana asked.

'You will see!' said Dad cheerfully.

Last time, they'd turned left and walked to the stream. But this time they turned right, then left, then right again, then straight, a right, a right, a left. Kiana stopped keeping track. Anyway, she didn't have any bread crumbs like Gretel and Hansel.

At last, they reached a grove of deciduous trees. By now, everyone was sweating enough to have filled that stream up twice, Subhir suspected.

'Right here,' Ma beamed. Their smiles had now started looking sinister, given they rarely appeared.

Nani removed her phone and started scrolling. Music piped out.

'Nani, we said no . . . ' Subhir said, as Kiana groaned.

'We know!' Dad, his grin getting even wider. 'Hence the permission.'

'Special one!' Nani added.

'We are going to do a rain dance!' Ma said. 'Like in the movies!' She struck a pose and said, 'Music!'

Subhir and Kiana wished that the sun would do its thing and just evaporate them right there and then. This was one of the worst ideas they had ever heard, and that too after a week of terrible ideas.

'We absolutely will not,' Kiana and Subhir said firmly in unison. They crossed their arms, and stood next to each other, as if they could physically stop this from happening.

'This is a ridiculous idea,' Subhir said.

'It's not even an idea!' Kiana said. 'It's a ridiculous thing you have got from watching too many Bollywood films and writing them. I keep telling you to watch cartoons instead. They are way smarter.'

'Hey, we watch documentaries too!' Ma protested. 'And your dad has even co-written one.'

'Also,' Subhir was grasping at straws now, 'if you dance, you will get sweaty, and then you will need a bath again. That's three baths! Imagine such a waste of water during this time.'

'We can't do that to our city's water reservoirs,' Kiana quickly agreed. 'No, never! We have to do our duty as citizens.'

'We will dance and it will rain, and then water will not be a problem. That is our duty as citizens,' Dad pointed out in a very matter-of-fact tone. He couldn't understand why his generally smart children were not understanding such a basic thing.

Since when did dancing become a citizen duty? Subhir wondered.

'And I made a baarish playlist!' Nani looked giddy with delight. She brandished her phone again. It was even fully charged for the occasion. And the songs downloaded, in case of network failure.

'We've been practising,' Ma said.

'No wonder Nani's back is aching!' Subhir cried.

'It's good exercise,' Nani said and pressed play. 'My back will be fine.'

Just then, a jeep came trundling in. A forest guard hopped out and ran towards them. 'Ma'am, sir, ma'am,' he said, turning all around. He wasn't sure whom to address. 'Permission's been withdrawn, sir,' he said, finally looking at Dad.

'Nooooo!' Ma let out a long wail and strode up to him with the paper. 'But why? It took us ages to get it.'

'The Forest Department thought you wanted to do a rain WATCH. No dancing allowed, ma'am. You know that. You are a regular here. You tell people off for littering. And you want to dance?'

'Now look here, young man.' Nani stepped in front, her

face an angry cloud. She was about to launch into a tirade, when Subhir and Kiana quickly intervened.

'We're so, so sorry,' they looked at his badge, 'Karim Uncle. We're going. Now.' Subhir elbowed Kiana. With the power of their newly acquired sibling communicating ability, Kiana made puppy eyes at the forest guard uncle.

'I will drop you to the gate.' Karim Uncle nodded. He beckoned them to sit in the jeep.

'We can walk,' Dad scowled.

'Yes, my back is sore,' Nani said. 'Cannot sit in a jeep.'

'Instructions, sir, ma'am,' Karim Uncle said. He looked at the children pleadingly while mopping his forehead with a daintily embroidered handkerchief.

Dad's scowl deepened.

'They don't believe you won't dance,' Karim Uncle added, staring straight ahead.

'Nor do we,' Kiana said, climbing into the jeep. Subhir shook his head and followed. But he stopped. A frog hopped off from the jeep. Subhir politely waited for him to pass before he climbed in as well.

CHAPTER 10
Then It Got Worse

'I can't believe they don't trust us.'

'We had permission. We are not rule breakers.'

'This was for the greater good.'

'Who confuses the word "dance" with "watch"?'

'I should really just go home now. I'm so done with this.'

'Absolutely your fault. Thanks to your terrible handwriting.'

'Well, you're the doctor. You should have atrocious handwriting, but you don't!'

'Excuse me for not being a cliché! All the chemists love me.'

The three grown-ups were striding up the path to Decent Apartments, complaining like the time when Subhir and his friends had got caught red-handed putting a dead cockroach in the biology teacher's desk.

Subhir's knees were weak with relief. He couldn't believe what fate the forest and he had just escaped. Whew! Kiana too looked pale, but less wobbly than when their parents had announced their noble intention to do a choreographed rain dance.

'I am hungry,' he told Kiana.

'What's new?'

'It's the nerves. I am so relieved Karim Uncle came just in time,' Subhir said. 'We should thank him. I say we take some doughnuts for him. Ooh, speaking of doughnuts, I think we should have some yummy—'

The grown-ups had stopped.

There was silence as they stared at the little grove of trees in Decent Apartments. Subhir and Kiana stared at it too, their hearts plummeting to their feet.

As one, Ma, Dad and Nani walked into the grove. They looked at each other and nodded.

Nani whipped out her phone, scrolled and pressed play.

Subhir and Kiana stepped back in horror. Ma shook a leg. Dad shook another leg. Nani moved a shoulder, then another shoulder. And as one, they began to twirl. To move. To shake like they had lost their keys (or their marbles). They were dancing. Right there. In the middle of Decent Apartments. Where anyone and everyone could see them. And film them.

The brother and sister held hands. They wanted to run away but they couldn't bring themselves to stop staring at the horror in front of them.

As the grown-ups danced, it attracted attention. First, Makhija Aunty and André poked their heads out of their first-floor window. Then Mr Mafatlal, who hated being called Uncle, slowly dragged his chair from the clubhouse

to the grove and sat down to watch. The couple who lived at D 601 called security to find out what was happening, so the security guards abandoned their post to answer their important question.

Divya, Rohan, Imaad, Gareth and Sahiba ran down from their play area, and stared in awe. André picked up their phone and began filming, ignoring Makhija Aunty's gestures to stop. Nani's Walking Group buddies ground to a halt.

And yet, the three grown-ups kept dancing. They danced like no one was watching. But EVERYONE was watching. Even Catrina, who had stepped out for an evening walk, stopped to stare. Kiana swore that she looked as embarrassed as them, if not more.

Finally, Subhir said, 'At least Nani can dance.'

'That's really not the point,' Kiana said, weakly.

'I know, but you know.'

'I know.'

'Um . . . Should we join them?'

Kiana looked at her brother in shock. Subhir, if he could have looked at himself, would have also looked at himself in shock. What had he just said! He pressed his hands to his mouth to stop more words from coming out.

'What fun!' Sahiba shrieked.

Subhir and Kiana started. They peered at their extremely embarrassing grown-ups. Ma was laughing, her face looking up at the skies. Nani's face was creased with smiles all over again. Dad was whooping with joy.

'It does look like fun,' Makhija Aunty hollered. 'Wait for us.' She grabbed André's hand, and ran down to join the circle. Mr Mafatlal began tapping his leg, and twirling his cane. The security guards also began to do a little jig, and the Walking Group suddenly became the Dancing Group.

Subhir and Kiana realized the wisdom in 'if you can't

fight it, join in'.

Together, with their friends, they stepped into the circle and let loose all their pent-up feelings of the last few months.

They danced, jumped, shouted, hollered, twirled, spun, bopped, leapt, frolicked. It felt like hours, though it was probably just a few songs (so far, 'Chak dhoom dhoom', 'Ghanan ghanan' and 'Ab ke sawaan').

Ma danced up to her children and kissed their foreheads. 'You watch, it will—'

As she said it, Kiana felt a drop on her arm. She brushed it off, certain that it was sweat.

Then Subhir felt one on his head.

As did Dad, Nani and Ma.

Before they could say chatak, they were all feeling drops of water.

A whoop went across the group. 'It's raining,' André said, a tad obviously. The security guards too began to dance faster, limbs moving faster than a black mamba.

'Don't stop,' Dad yelled. 'It needs to rain more. Not just drizzle.' He ran around the trees looking wildly for the cuckoo. 'She must be here somewhere. Where are you!'

Nani put out an arm and felt a cooling drop fall on it slowly. She itched to text her friends, but then she remembered: #YOLO. And anyway, the music was playing on her phone.

Subhir couldn't believe it. He just couldn't. If someone had told him that his family would make it rain, he would have offered to eat his hat. Or rather, his dad's kale salad. But now it was really happening, and he didn't care how it had happened. He jumped up and down and turned to Kiana.

Kiana, who was just standing and staring at everyone.

'This is wild!' He hopped over to her. He finally understood why grasshoppers travelled like this. And toads. And frogs! Hopping was so much fun.

Kiana nodded. Clearly, the shock of her family's achievement had gotten to her as well. 'But—'

'We're going to go viral,' Subhir said. 'Hope someone's filming it. Oh no, Makhija Aunty told André not to shoot.'

Kiana shook her head.

Subhir slowed down from his frog hopping as she pointed up. He looked up as well. 'What?'

She waggled a finger.

'WHAT?'

'There's no cloud.'

'I know! It's miracle rain!' Subhir said. 'From our family's wishes.'

Kiana sighed. Her brother's stupidity made her snap out of her reverie. 'It's not miracle rain.'

'Huh?'

'It's not raining,' she whispered. 'There's not a single cloud in the sky. In fact . . .' Kiana stepped out of the grove, dragging her brother with her. She then added, 'Well, I guess it is a kind of rain? It's cicada rain.'

'It's what?' Subhir asked.

'It's cicadas,' Kiana said. 'They're peeing on us. Well, now on them.'

'EWWW!'

Subhir hastily stepped further away and peered up the trees. He couldn't see them but they were there. Cicadas. A bug who loves to pee when it's warm. They can pee stronger and faster than humans and even elephants!

'We must have woken them up with all that singing and dancing,' Kiana added, helpfully. 'It's really just tree sap that they drink, so it's not actually gross, you know. It's just—' she fumbled for the right word, '—excreted tree sap. They pee a lot when it's hot.'

The explanation continued but it did not help Subhir at all. He felt like he had been forced to learn trigonometry in Shakespearean language. 'So they just spray it on to those below?' he asked. He felt both grossed out and annoyed. He imagined the cicadas having a good laugh at the silly humans below them. Now he definitely did need a shower. He shuddered. He sniffed his arm covertly. *Did the pee smell*, he wondered, *or was that him?* He was anyway constantly sweaty and smelly, so he couldn't figure it out.

'But it's called rain, and even blessings!' Kiana said. 'So, you know, it did rain. I mean, different kind but . . . oh well.'

'Should we tell them?' Subhir asked.

They took in the sight of the dancing humans in front of them.

'What's the point?' Kiana asked.

CHAPTER 11

Cicadas aka *Cicadoidea*

CHAPTER 12

The Jacobin cuckoo aka the Pied cuckoo aka the Chatak aka the *Clamator jacobinus*

The chatak veered to her left, her internal radar guiding her. She wasn't sure why but the timing felt off. The weather had been strange. It had felt too early to leave her last home. And somehow, she didn't feel quite ready to show up at her next destination.

If she could have shrugged her feathered shoulders, she would have.

Instead, she thought about her last home. The one she had left behind. She was still annoyed with the male chatak, not sure why she had listened to his persuasive chirps. She gave him the side-eye.

Meanwhile, the male chatak was taking a quick rest stop by a lake. Hmmm, the lake looked a bit less full. Anyway, it didn't really matter as long as he could check his reflection out. Hello, good-looking. His crest was as spiffy as when he had left the southern part of Africa. He chirped a bit to himself. He needed to keep his voice sound for mating calls once back home. Also, he needed to keep up the looks for the welcoming committee of twitchers who would be eagerly waiting for them.

He fluffed his wings and took to the skies again.

At last, land ahoy! The female chatak could see the Arabian Sea glinting blue-green and then grey, as she neared the shores of Mumbai.

She was exhausted. What a long haul, past the talons of the sparrowhawk. But her bulbul mama had trained her to spot the raptor from miles away, and she had quickly hidden.

Together, she and the male chatak swooped down to the land. Legend had it that it looked less green and more grey every time the species returned.

They were late this year. It was the male chatak's fault. But he had heard on a podcast by one of the humans that it's fashionable to make a late entry. And the cuckoos are nothing if not fashionable.

Which is why he had spent the last few weeks convincing every single pied cuckoo to leave their shores just a little later. He explained something called climate change, which made their eyes glaze over. But he was charming, and so they finally had agreed.

Now, he flapped his wings harder. Piu, piu piu, he called. There was a throng of human beings dancing and waving their hands in the air right by a grove of trees. Right on time, the welcome committee was cheering them on. The female chatak called. She turned right—she was first going to Beauty Van. She was hungry and thirsty. The male hoped his crest was as jaunty as before and not tired from the trip. He called loudly. But no one heard over the jhankaar beats.

A lone boy, a girl and a cat witnessed the arrival of the two birds. The boy and girl held each other's hands tightly, while the cat looked bored. One of them told the other that it was indeed the cuckoo. She would have danced, but she really did not want to go back into the grove. The other couldn't understand what the fuss had been about, over such a tiny black-and-white bird. He'd rather eat an Oreo. He now wanted an Oreo, so he dragged his sister inside their concrete nest. The cat too stalked after them. She could smell fish.

ACKNOWLEDGEMENTS

A chorus of cicadas made this book happen
Thank you:

A cluck for editor Aparna Kapur for giving me the O in POFFS, for believing in the story, and for general awesomeness.

A coo for publisher Tina Narang for making me part of the Power Poffs set.

A hoot for Canato Jimo for his happy illustrations.

A roar for Deepanjana Pal and Sudeshna Shome Ghosh for reading and listening to my rants, Vena Kapoor for meticulous fact checking, Nimmy Chacko for careful reading, Lavanya Karthik, Amrita Dutta and Menaka Raman for their excellent company; Radha Rangarajan and Rajiv Eipe for front-seat bird watching, and Kanishka Gupta for all the fine print.

And a chirp for the cicadas of Pench who rained on us and gave me the story idea.

ABOUT THE AUTHOR

Bijal Vachharajani stumbles a lot, mostly because she's not looking where she's going she's usually peering at clouds and birds or squinting at spiders and mantises. She's the author of multiple planet-friendly award-winning books including *When Fairyland Lost Its Magic*. She is now a certified climate worrier.

ABOUT THE ILLUSTRATOR

Canato Jimo is a picture-book maker from Nagaland. He currently lives in Bangalore chasing deadlines as an art director. He moonlights as a musician, loves to guzzle tea and pop bubble wrap, and is a recovering stationery addict.